ONE COOL CAT!

SUSANNAH CORBETT

DAVID ROBERTS

EGMONT

First published in Great Britain 2012 by Egmont UK Limited. 239 Kensington High Street, London W8 6SA

ISBN 978 1 4052 3035 3

Text copyright © Susannah Corbett 2012   Illustrations copyright © David Roberts 2012

www.egmont.co.uk

www.susannahcorbett.co.uk

Printed and bound in Singapore

A CIP catalogue record for this title is available from the British Library.

10 9 8 7 6 5 4 3 2 1

EGMONT
We bring stories to life

Shoe

BLOOMS

umbrella

TOY

For Dan, Lily and Elena S.C.   To Mr and Mrs Roberts-Maloney D.R.

On a long, hot, lazy afternoon, the sun
bounced off the bright wet paint on a shop, and
baked the shimmering pavements of the street.

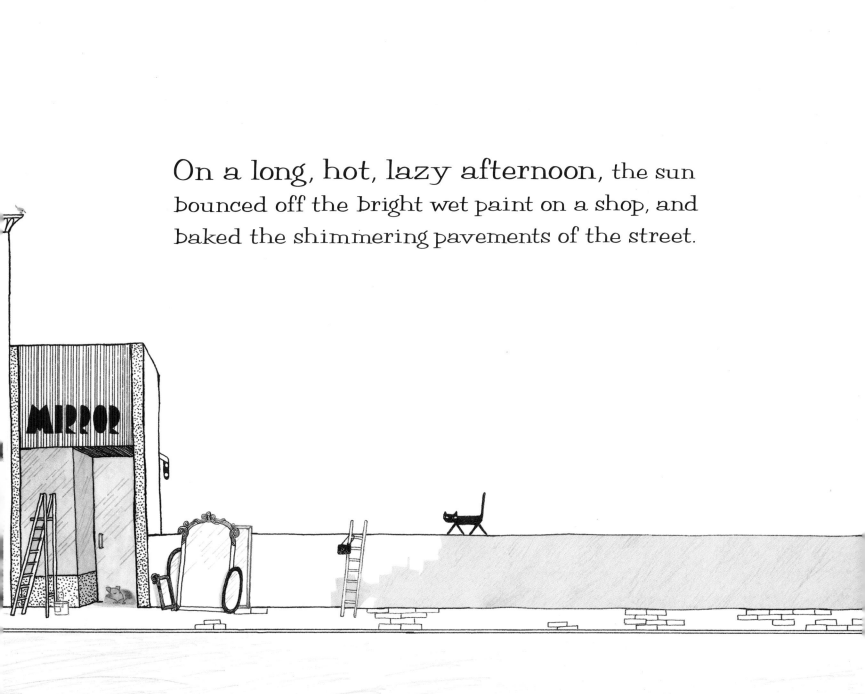

A white cat slinked down the street.

He sneered at a dog
        lounging in the shadowy doorway of a shop

and preened in the mirrors stacked up on the pavement.

Pouncing on a pebble,

he **batted** it towards his reflection.

"**Ooo**, you didn't want to do that," said a black cat sitting nearby on the wall.

"You've cracked a mirror. Terrible **bad luck** that is," he explained. "You could cut yourself."

"Listen, friend," snapped the white cat, "when you look this good, you don't need luck!"

OW, Miaow

– he was ONE COOL CAT!

The dog
got up,

sniffed at the
cracked mirror,

and pricked
his nose.

The black cat padded
along the wall.

The white cat went to
play with some leaves
skittering in a breeze
at the foot of the ladder.

They watched
each other
for a while,

as only cats can.

"**Don't go under it,**" said the black cat.

"**Terrible bad luck** if you go under a ladder. Something could fall on you."

"Oh pur-lees," smirked the white cat, as he rubbed his cheeks on the ladder's smooth wood.

"Use your brain. I'm nowhere near it.

Look pal, when you're this smart, you don't **need** luck!"

The dog sniffed
at the ladder

and looked up,

just as the breeze
blew a drip of paint
into his eye.

"**Oooh,** I wouldn't step on those **cracks,**"

murmured the black cat,

"just in case."

"Just in case of **what?**"
laughed the white cat.
"No, don't tell me,
in case
a very small
volcano
erupts
under my paws!"

The dog's eyebrows

wriggled like caterpillars

as he eyed one of the cracks
in the pavement.

The
white
cat
cackled

as he

danced

on
the
cracks.

The black cat watched him,
as only cats can.

"I know," shrieked the white cat.

"Better not step on the crack in case a HUGE beanstalk shoots up

the sky!"

into

and CATapults me

WITTY, KITTY

– he was ONE COOL CAT!

"You
could
trip,"

said the black cat.

"Trip!"

screamed the white cat,
holding his sides.

"Trip... cats don't trip."

He laughed so much
he fell over . . .

and

knocked

the mirror...

...that smashed

on

the

ladder

...that *shocked* the painter...

who

dropped

the

brush . . .

that hit the dog.

The dog turned
on the white cat.
He snarled,
bared his fangs
and lunged at him.

But the white cat
was too fast.
He sprang away
from the dog
and up,
over the wall.

"Nice try, pooch," he cried,

"but when you're **this quick,** you don't **need . . ."**

YEEEO

The black cat watched, as only cats can,
as the white cat was carried
down the tracks
and out of the town,
wailing all the way.

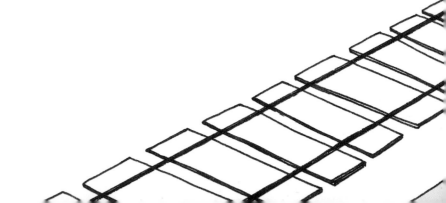

WWWRRRrrrrrrrLLLLiiiiiiii

The dog turned to the black cat and smiled . . .

"WRONG,
GONE
– he was
ONE FOOL CAT!"